Time Pieces

for
Trumpet

Music through the Ages in 3 Volumes

Volume 3

**Selected and arranged by
Paul Harris and John Wallace**

**The Associated Board of
the Royal Schools of Music**

CONTENTS

Time Pieces for Trumpet

Volume 3

1588 Branle des Sabots

from *Orchesographie*

Thoinot Arbeau
(1520–1595)

AB 2494

1625 Very Old Celebrated Trumpet Tune

arr. Nathaniel Gow
(1763–1831)

AB 2494

1651 Hit and Miss

Anon.

from *The English Dancing Master*

1680 Second Air de Trompette

Marc-Antoine Charpentier
(1634–1704)

AB 2494

Trio

D.C. al Fine

1695 The Red House

from *The English Dancing Master*

Anon.

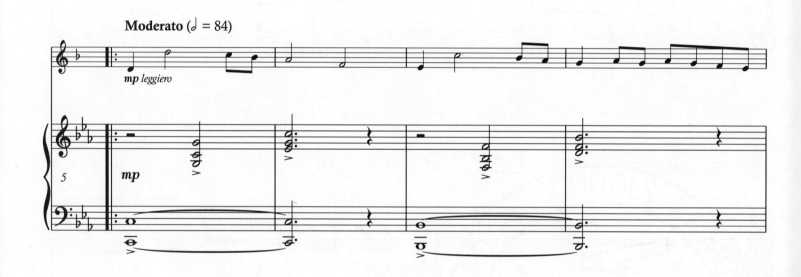

1700 Prelude

Marc-Antoine Charpentier
(1634–1704)

1704 March

Archangelo Corelli
(1653–1713)

* A more authentic performance may be achieved by double dotting where appropriate, throughout.

AB 2494

1722 Impertinence

George Frideric Handel
(1685–1759)

1740 The Shepherds

Louis-Claude Daquin
(1694–1772)

AB 2494

1750 Bugle Horn

Anon.

1770 Largo

Thomas Erskine, 4th Earl of Kelly
(*fl.*1750–1780)

1805 Romanze

Johann Nepomuk Hummel
(1778–1837)

AB 2494

1817 The Monk of Bangor's March

Ludwig van Beethoven
(1770–1827)

1851 Andantino

Louis Köhler
(1820–1886)

1861 Johnny get your hair cut

American traditional song

AB 2494

1894 Humoresque

Antonín Dvořák
(1841–1904)

1934 A New Year Carol

from *Friday Afternoons*, Op. 7

Benjamin Britten
(1913–1976)

1944 Waltz

from *Six Children's Pieces*, Op. 69

Dmitri Shostakovich
(1906–1975)

1991 Lounge Lizard

Paul Harris

1995 Trooping the Colour

Paul Harris

AB 2494

Music origination by
Barnes Music Engraving Ltd, East Sussex
Printed by Halstan & Co Ltd, Amersham, Bucks, England